BIRDSONGS OF LOVE & DESPAIR

Stories from Varanasi

BIRDSONGS OF LOVE & DESPAIR

Stories from Varanasi

Vivek Nath Mishra

HAWAKAL

HAWAKAL

Published by Hawakal Publishers
185 Kali Temple Road, Nimta, Kolkata 700049
India

Email info@hawakal.com
Website www.hawakal.com

First edition: June, 2019

Edited by Sarbajit Sarkar

Cover photography: Plabon Das
Cover design: Bitan Chakraborty

ISBN: 978-93-87883-67-3

Price: INR 250 | USD 8.99

For
my father *Shri Nagendra Prasad Mishra*
&
mother *Late Indo Devi*

I would like to express my special thanks of gratitude to my family members, *Dr. Banibrata Mahanta*, professor of English at Banaras Hindu University and all the editors of *Hawakal* for being there and helping me as and when I needed.

Some of these stories have appeared earlier in *The Hindu, Muse India, Queen mob's Teahouse.*

CONTENTS

ANKLET

Every time she saw me in the street she would ask, "How's your child?" inevitably I would say "naughty", just to amuse myself. As a matter of fact I didn't have any child till then, though I had been married for four years. It was surprising for a lady, bounded by old traditions, to believe that a marriage could last without a child for four years.

I remember how Usha first approached us for a job. I was a kid then. She was then newly married. She always had a smile on her face and wore fake jewelry. She used to only do the dishes and wipe the floors, but stayed back till late in the night and did whatever she was told to do.

She looked grotesque with her made up face. I guess she was thirty years old and married late. Usha would tell my mother sometimes about the ordeals her parents had gone through to get her married. They spent all their savings to pay a huge dowry.

She used to say, her husband was loving and compassionate. She missed no opportunity to praise him. However, my mother knew her husband already: he was grumpy, had a stern face and undoubtedly was a drunkard. She had seen him many times on the street in a lungi and a dirty shirt. There would always be tobacco in his mouth. His teeth had become reddish due to chewing tobacco all the time. He would smoke a bidi outside his small shanty on a rickshaw. He had a rickshaw but he hardly used it to earn some money. My mother had never seen him giving someone a ride. She had seen him many times outside a liquor shop fighting at the counter. He was found many times completely drunk lying on the side of the road. My mother was sure that he was drinking with Usha's hard earned money. My mother would always say that Usha's husband had a demonic laugh. One of our neighbors had told mother that Usha's husband used to torture his parents for money till they both died.

Once I heard my mother talking to my father about Usha's husband. They must have thought I was asleep. I used to sleep with them during those days. My mother was telling my father about how worried she was for Usha. She believed that Usha was a good lady who worked hard for the welfare of her family. Everyone knew that Usha's husband was much older than Usha and probably she was his second wife.

Usha desired to live a good life. Whenever she would find me reading from a book or writing something in my notebook she would come and stand beside. Books seemed to attract her a lot. She used to dust them with reverence. She used to dust the books with a separate cloth and never used the one which she used to wipe other things. While dusting if a book fell down she would immediately pick it up and touch it to her forehead. She said her parents didn't have money or else she could have studied in school, wore better clothes and would have got a job in some office by now.

She remained shy initially but after a few months requested me to teach her. She wished to read and write. "If only I could write my name," she would say. I began teaching her but it was a hard task and I thought she would be bored in a few days. But her determination was quite impressive. She didn't give up. She kept trying hard. There was a marked change in her behavior. Earlier she would keep humming the movie songs. Those melodies she picked up from roadside tobacco shops but later she kept repeating the Hindi alphabets. Had she been to the school from the beginning she would have been a very good student, I thought.

In a few months, Usha learned to write her name. She wrote large wobbly letters. She wrote it everywhere. My father had bought a separate notebook for her but while wiping the floor she would write her name on a piece of newspaper or any paper she found. She looked so elated after she learned to write her name. It gave her eyes a bright shine. She looked happier than before. Anyone could notice a sense of accomplishment in her eyes now. But she never took the notebook to her shanty. When I asked her for the reason she told me that her husband wouldn't approve that. "He doesn't know reading and writing. How would he accept that his wife should know," she had said it as if it was obviously understood.

"Your husband is a bad person, no?" I asked her one day and she looked rather taken aback.

"Who said master? He's a very nice person. He keeps me like a queen," she had said.

The queen, who worked in other houses, cleaned their dirty dishes and wiped floor to afford a life.

For Usha, her husband had every good quality one would look for in a husband. In order not to hurt her sentiments, my mother would nod in assent to each of her exuberant commendations.

But for how long can truth be disguised? Soon, Usha started coming in with a new bruise on her body each day, sometimes on her face, sometimes on her back, sometimes on her shoulders. However, for an Indian woman, her husband is her dignity and she would always give new excuses. Sometimes she would say she fell off a ladder, sometimes she would say she had this habit of walking in her sleep and bumped into something. However, no excuse ever seemed relevant or credible.

But what a strong lady she was! The stoic smile which was her trademark always remained unaltered there.

How can I ever trust a smile!

One day my mother lost her calm and blurted out in rage. "Why don't you lodge a police complaint against your husband who beats you daily"!

Tears started to rebel against her smile. Her smile was trying vigorously to restrain the tears. It was like a battle. A battle she lost to tears, which rolled down her cheeks. "But I am just unable to conceive; how could I blame him when the fault is mine?" she said with quivering lips.

After this, she suddenly disappeared and never came in again. I was in high school then and after waiting for three days my mother put me on a task of finding her. However, I was told she had left her husband's house and gone back to her parents in the village. I thought my mother would be very disappointed hearing this as she would have to look for a new maid. But she heaved a sigh of relief and said she deserved better.

Many years went by. I was a married man now. I was working as a teacher in a small school and was a struggling writer. I would wash myself diligently daily early in the morning and would ignore my mother's pleading to do the prayers, like most of us do in our beaming youth. Not a speck of dirt could be found over my clothes. I would part my hair carefully, leaving not a single strand left unsettled on my head. My shoes would always be spotlessly clean. After this daily routine, I would take my motorbike to collect my friend Dinesh who worked in the same school with me.

It was at that time when I saw Usha again after so many years. She might not have been very old but the wrinkles told another story. She walked slowly and limping. This was the first time she had asked me about my child, as if she knew already that I was married, and after that she inquired daily, almost each time she met me.

Later Dinesh told me that Usha was working in his house. Why she did not come to our house again was quite understandable. She might have been embarrassed because of her husband's deplorable behavior. Whenever she found me waiting there for

Dinesh she would come and start talking, I tried to avoid her each time but never succeeded.

After this she disappeared again. I got to know about it after months when Dinesh told me that he was looking for a maid. When I asked for Usha's whereabouts, he said she had not been seen for months. It didn't concern me much and I forgot about it, assuming that she was at her parents' again.

One Sunday morning I was having a cup of tea in my comfortable rattan chair in my large balcony. The sun was rising ahead of me, the sky was turning orange, birds were chirping in the bougainvillea bush that had grown rampantly and clutched anything on the way to come up. It was a peaceful and serene morning.

I had just started to read the newspaper when I heard a desperate knock on my door. What a nuisance, I mumbled, irritated by the incessant knocks that didn't stop until I opened the gate. I was expecting a familiar face, but there was a stranger who looked like had come straight out of his bed, with a swollen face and disheveled look.

Satish! Are you Satish, asked the boy, in a hurry?

Yes? I asked with curiosity.

The lady who worked at your place wants to see you right now. She is on her death bed. Come right away, he said with authority.

I went inside, took my jacket and left with the boy.

I passed many narrow streets. Blackish water with an unbearable foul smell in the open gutter was running along the street. I felt suffocated. Filth was scattered everywhere. There was the foul smell of animal excrement lingering in the air. I found no dustbins anywhere. Little children with running noses and scruffy hair were playing on the street, and their protruding bones and poor health showed their parents' state of penury. All were almost bare-bodied; the clothes they wore had either no buttons or were torn. I had never seen such scenes before in my life. Even the mongrels there found my clean clothes and body odor strange and barked at me.

We stopped in front of a shanty. The roof was of corrugated tin, with many holes. The thought of living in such a house during the ferocious monsoon season sent a shiver down my spine.

I bent low and entered through a small gate. There was Usha in front of me, lying on the floor as there was no bed. There was just a thin mat, with her meager belongings, a few utensils, and a few clothes. Her room felt cold and damp.

She was lying there motionless, but after a while she fluttered a little, opened her eyes with effort and recognized me immediately. Her stoic smile was back on her face.

However, she said nothing, just beckoned me to sit closer and took out something from under her pillow. It was a gleaming anklet, shimmering bright, made of silver. She thrust the anklet into my hands and spoke in a shaking voice, "This is for your child".

I felt ashamed, not knowing what to say. I just said I cannot take it. She didn't ask for a reason. I think she knew now as I saw tears in her eyes.

Don't return it, she pleaded. I bless you with a child, my son; she spoke softly and held my hands tightly.

I felt her frail body didn't have much physical strength, but she had a powerful soul.

That day, for the first time in my life it came to my mind that a child is a blessing indeed.

The next day I heard of Usha's death. I came to know that her husband attended her funeral, the only good thing he ever did to her.

Usha had left this world, but left her blessing with me.

This little girl, Usha, who kept bothering me as I was writing this story, just loves her anklet more than anything else.

OF WINDOWS AND CAGES

The deal was already done but he was not informed. Had he been told before it was settled, he would have resisted it. He had written the house in his sons' names long ago for he had wanted to free himself of everything and didn't want anything in his name. He thought so to relieve himself of all the burdens. He wanted to live a life more on a lighter note after retiring from the long teaching job. He had taught history in a government school for almost forty years without taking many leaves. He had two sons both working for a corporate company. They would leave the house early in the morning at eight and come back late in the night. He detested such life. Even the idea of such a life gave him shivers. He often wondered why his sons earned so much money when they had no time even to spend it. They worked even on holidays and weekends. He wondered whether his sons ever missed watching a sunset or a sunrise. He wondered whether they could ever get a chance to feel the serenity of it, whether they had observed the beauty of a placidly flowing river.

He would remain in his room with his books. As his sons came late in the night and mostly remained busy with their work at home too, there was not much interaction between them. Books and proximity to nature were the only things he desired in his life anymore. He loved reading books of philosophy, especially Krishnamurthy. He used to visit the Krishnamurthy foundation at Rajghat when Krishnamurthy lived there. He never missed any of his public discourses. Daily in the evening, he would put on his Khadi kurta, comb his hair neatly, and take out his old bicycle to peddle through the streets and shortcuts up to the foundation. Sometimes, he would walk all the way to Rajghat from his place. He preferred to walk along the river Ghats. He was born there in Varanasi and he knew a short route for every place. He took pride that he knew all the streets. "A true Banarasi is the one who knows a shortcut for every place," he would quote proudly. "These narrow streets are veins of Varanasi. These are not only streets. These streets, these lanes and by-lanes keep Varanasi alive. Life and vitality runs through these narrow, crooked streets." He would say often. But lately after the death of Krishnamurthy he stopped going there at the foundation. "With him went away the energy of that place," he had said after reading the news of his death in the newspaper.

In the middle of his house there was an open courtyard. His wife had planted a guava tree in the middle. His sons had wanted it all to be cemented while he was against that. He wanted at least a square foot of earth without cement in his house. Firstly, he wanted the whole courtyard to remain without cement but he failed to persuade his sons.

"Where would I plant the guava tree?" he had asked his son.

"But father it will create mud when it rains," his son had said. "What is the use of the rain when we can't smell it on parched earth!" He thought.

In winter afternoons, he would take out his cane arm chair out in the courtyard and read under the pleasant sun for hours. He had looked for that rattan arm chair everywhere in the city. The shopkeepers at furniture shops had disappointed him every time, telling him that those belonged to an older generation. Now no one has time to relax in a cane chair after all. He had looked for it everywhere and finally had to give a shopkeeper some money in advance to make one for him. When his elder son had noticed the new arm chair, he gave him a harsh look.

"The house is already so small, it already lacks space and now where would we keep this arm chair?" his elder son remarked.

He was in love with his house. The courtyard in the middle allowed him some peace, away from the noise of neighbor's television.

He was concerned about his son's different opinions. However, he didn't realise his sons could sell the house one day. He had so many memories in this house; how could he part with it just because it had become older with time?

His sons managed a good amount of money by selling the house and now they were buying a flat on the twenty-fifth floor of a complex outside of the city. They had also decided to sell almost everything in the old house. They were determined to furnish the new flat with everything new; no old junk they would take there.

"So, are they willing to take you and me to their new house? Are we not old? What if they reject us later?

What if we don't match with the look of new house?"
he had asked his wife one night and his wife had looked
away uncomfortably, unable to find an answer. She
sobbed in a corner. It was the same house where she
had seen the first sunrays with her husband. She was
brought to that house after marriage. How diligently
she busied herself all day to keep the house neat and
clean.

The house had been a big problem for his sons.
It was in a narrow alley, which made it difficult for even
a tricycle to pass through. His sons wanted to buy cars
but that wasn't possible when they lived in that house.
The senior went into his room; this had been his room
since he was born. He started running his hands over
the wall surfaces, and over the books he had collected
over time. Those one and a half feet thick walls kept
the house pretty warm in the winters and cool in the
sweltering summers. He never bought an air-conditioner.
"My house is already air-conditioned, why waste money
only to cut oneself off from nature?" he used to ask.
His windows would be open through all the seasons. It
was like a big television screen where he could watch
the soothing rain coming down heavily after a scorching
season. Now, the new flat they were to move into would
be fully air-conditioned. It wouldn't let him open the
windows.

He looked at the murals he had drawn in his
free time. He had painted the ghats of Varanasi on those
walls, as if he had brought in a part of Varanasi to his
room. He never bathed in the tiny bathroom at his home;
it never gave him the freshness he wanted. Even in the
cold winter he would wake up early in the morning and
walk down to the ghats, and take several dips in the
Ganga. Then he would take a pot of Ganga water and
march down the street briskly, straight to the Siva temple,

where he would pour it on the Siva lingam. The temple was only a few blocks from the Ganga.

When he would return to his home, a bull would be waiting there for him. It was his pet bull and he had named it Nandi. It was a giant in size but was as sedate as a turtle, and it strolled through the crooked streets all day with the speed of a turtle. It would forage for food here and there, poking its head into every refuse bin for leftovers.

The old house was one among only a few where it would get a loaf of bread. The bull would be there right at the door, and wouldn't let him enter the house until it was fed. He would ask his wife to throw a loaf of bread from the window in the kitchen and would feed Nandi with his own hands. After eating, the bull would move away from the door. He always remained proud that Nandi came only to his house, although it was true that it came to his house only because he fed it regularly. Yet he believed the bull had chosen him and his house. His mother had told him early on in his life that his house would be a home in the real sense only if love and respect found a home in it. This had been his routine for many years.

There was a small hole on the northern side of the wall of his house where a sparrow had built a nest. A pair of sparrows hatched eggs in it round the year. Every few months the baby sparrows would come out and hop around. Every time his sons argued with him about it and tried to get the hole plastered, he fought on behalf of the birds. "And where would the birds go — for a slight beautification?" he would ask. He refused to get it plastered. This hole was there for many years now.

Beside his front door he had built a small wooden box with his own hands, and spread a ragged blanket in it. A mother dog with its puppies slept in it, curled up and snuggling with one another in warmth.

Now all of it had to change; they had to move. It wasn't only about the house; it was also about his lifestyle, which had to be altered. He climbed down his narrow spiral stairs and recalled what trouble it had posed whenever they had to move something big in size up or down. Finally, they were rid of the trouble. Now they would use a lift to climb up to the twenty-fifth floor. No Nandi would come and obstruct the path at his doorway. No dog would sleep beside his door. Stray dogs are not allowed in the big complexes. Sparrows wouldn't come hopping for grain.

The day they had to move out from the old house, a small wagon came rattling to his house to carry a few important household goods. He kept everything near to his heart in his bag, and with a drooping countenance was about to leave. Hardly had he reached the corner of the street than he turned around and looked back once again for the last time, as if something had beckoned him back. He saw that his neighbor was filling up the hole where the sparrow had built its nest, with a piece of brick. He ran towards him to ask, "What are you doing, it's somebody's home." The man turned slightly towards him and said with disdain, "It's not your house anymore. I have talked to the owner of the house. These filthy, noisy birds need to move away. It's not a zoo; it's a residential area."

The sons were right behind him and they took him by his hand, "Father, leave it now, you're not a child." He couldn't say a word.

He wouldn't talk to his sons after moving into the flat. He stopped talking altogether. He started feeling lonely, and just kept staring out of the window. His gaze remained fixed on the pigeons all day. He would try to remain out of the house all day and would come back late at night. He would go to the Krishnamurthy foundation and spend his whole day in the silence room. They called it silence room to honor Krishnamurthy. Whenever Krishnamurthy came to Varanasi, he stayed there. He would watch the placid river flowing from the tall windows.

When his sons noticed that the new house was taking a toll on his health, they came into his room together one day with a wooden nest box. "Now you may have your birds here, father. It's not a very big issue. You shouldn't stress yourself out."

He took the nest box in his hand. It was a small, hut-shaped box painted green. It looked beautiful. A fragile smile flickered at the corner of his lips. It wasn't because he was happy. He laughed at the naiveté of his sons. Perhaps, they knew nothing about the emotions a creature as tiny as a sparrow possesses.

There's no space for a sparrow in the skyscrapers. Skyscrapers don't welcome them; in fact sparrows don't choose skyscrapers. They fly only a few meters above the ground. They are not the birds who fly high, and they don't touch the sky often. They like to remain near the ground just like him. He knew, that just like him, they wouldn't accept this as their home up on the twenty-fifth floor.

THE GARDENER

After many years, I found Sukhu uncle in a charity-run old age home. Age had crept on to his face, leaving deep wrinkles. His black, shiny eyes had sunk deeper than before. His receding hair had turned grey. His body had become emaciated and looked almost cadaverous; it seemed he had been starving for months.

I wouldn't have ever gone there, but my friend on his birthday wanted to distribute gifts in an old age home. He wanted me to go with him. He insisted so much that I had to go.

There I found him after a long time. He was looking unblinkingly at flowers, sitting by himself on a bench, for what seemed hours to me.

He was like that from the beginning, in love with plants, trees and flowers. It seemed he had not changed much from the inside. It was just the outer look that had become frail; he had withered in the course of time. Seeing him, my thoughts went back to a time when he was young and handsome.

Our house was somewhere in a labyrinth of old crooked streets near Lalita Ghat, where ruminating cows, contemplative and calm, used to move around, and meditative bulls leisurely roamed, and chased the cows amorously now and then. Red-faced macaques jumped from one building to another with their tails dangling in the air, always maneuvering to steal or snatch food, grooming or scratching themselves in their free time. Sadhus with matted hair and face painted with ash wandered, and dogs slept curled up near heaps of filth that was mounting by the day. The streets remained muddy and slippery, drenched in overflowing sewage water, and the smell of cow dung lingered in the air. The neighboring houses were dilapidated. Banyan tree shot up on any crevice or hole of old and decrepit walls, clutching and embracing till it crumbled down to earth.

In front of our house there was a small garden and Sukhu uncle was our gardener. He was obsessed with plants. It was our garden and Sukhu was just the gardener but he reigned there like a dictator. I think nobody could muster up the courage to come in his way in the matter of gardening decisions, not even the head of the family, my father. He was often ill-tempered, and always clad in a loin cloth. I don't know why my father never fired him. I didn't like his way of behaving and one day I was annoyed about something and went to complain about him. It so happened that I needed a flower for my school project. I went into the garden and was just sniffing the marigolds when he came and refused to let me pluck any. "Not from this garden. Why doesn't your teacher let you pluck few from his garden?" he said reproachfully. Blood rushed to my head, and I could hardly hold my anger. Immediately I ran to my father.

"Papa, please get a new gardener, what does he think about himself, he can't even let me pluck one flower," I said indignantly. My father was insouciant. "You wouldn't get a gardener like him," he said, smiling.

"You know he's so obstinate, he doesn't even let me touch his plants", I said.
"Come with me in the evening, I'll buy you a few from the market," my father said. But I didn't like the idea a bit.

Sukhu didn't like anyone intervening and chose his own spots to plant seedlings he brought from a nursery. He would flatter my father at the end of every month so he could get some money to buy plants for the garden. He would start nagging a week before the end of each month, telling my father how important it was to get new plants, manure and pots for the garden without procrastinating even for a single day. This is something he never forgot, although he was so forgetful about other things he didn't even remember his own pay date. He would always confuse between marigold and dahlia. He would call marigold dahlia and dahlia marigold.

I never found him pestering my father for his own payment; all he cared about was plants and trees. My father had built a small room for him in the corner of the garden. He would do his perfunctory cooking there and from his window keep an eye on the flowers.

My mother would sulk each morning when she would go for her prayers. "Such a big garden and so many flowers, but not even one I can offer to gods," she would say, while muttering her prayers. She would grunt in reply to my father's queries.

He was in my house even before my birth. Nobody knew from where he had come. When I asked my father he said, "He was a drifter, I think. He came and asked if he could take care of my garden and I agreed." Certainly he was a nomad as he never went away to visit his hometown or village. It seemed he had no relatives, no home, not much of belongings — except the garden he loved so much.

Everyone had a different take about his mysterious past. Some said he was a criminal and was actually hiding here. Some said he ran away from his house only to become a monk. My mother believed his presence in our house was a result of someone's evil or envious gaze. She presumed that his ominous presence would have some pretty serious repercussions someday.

His enthusiasm for plants and trees was exuberant. He took utmost care of every single plant. During summer he would spend all day under the margosa (neem) tree, lying there on a *khatiya*. He would tirelessly water all the plants and trees daily in the evening. His energy was exceptional.

I could dimly recall that evening when my mother asked Sukhu uncle to bring some vegetables from the market two blocks down the road. I was waiting for him to leave so I could pluck few marigolds in his absence just to tease him. I saw him leaving; the old iron door creaked on its hinges when he shut it behind him.

I kept waiting for him. Hours passed, night fell upon the city, but he never returned.

The next day my father wanted to lodge a police complaint, but my mother asked him to wait. "He's not a child. He must have stayed over with some old friends," she said.

Days turned into months but he didn't return. We started feeling Sukhu uncle's absence more than ever. My mother never admitted it, but she also missed him and remained sullen for weeks. She regretted her uncharitable remarks about him.

In a few weeks, our garden had lost its charm, the plants had withered and the trees had wilted. It seemed our garden was also silently weeping for its gardener.

After so many years I had found him in that old age home, still looking at plants unblinkingly. I went near him and called out his name; suddenly a man patted my shoulder from behind. "Do you know him?" he asked.

"Yes, he is Sukhu uncle. He was our gardener for years," I said.

"Can we have a word?" the man asked, and motioned me to a bench. I followed him. He pulled his long beard, lit a cigarette and offered me one, but I refused. Several minutes passed but he didn't say a word. It was as if a strange silence had descended on him.

"You wanted to talk about something," I broke the silence finally.

"He has Alzheimer's. He gets paranoid easily. Your talking might aggravate the problem. He has forgotten everything," the man said with a nonchalant air.

My jaw dropped, light faded from my face, I was stunned as if someone had struck me hard in my face. I sat there bewildered.

The man's voice echoed in my ears, and my heart reasoned: had he really forgotten everything!

I turned my eyes towards Sukhu uncle again. His thin body had a deadly calm about it. He was still looking at flowers. He was drooping like a wilted plant. Old age had set upon him. He has started withering too. However, that moment, I realized his love for plants and flowers had not died yet. He still looked smitten by flowers.

Perhaps, love is something a man never forgets, I thought.

LOST HOME

On the day of his retirement Narayan got out of bed early, before dawn. He had not slept the whole night, not even a wink, twirling restlessly in his bed. His dry eyes scorched and his face was swollen. It had drizzled all night intermittently. Wet clothes were scattered all over his bed, as he couldn't hang them out on the clothes line due to the rain. His room felt moist and there was a damp smell hanging in the air, his books had become soft from the moisture. Out of the window he saw dragonflies floating up and down, and small insects fluttering in the dim light of dawn. Sun was approaching horizon, lurking behind the heavy clouds which hung low in the sky. It would rain all day; as the forecast said, for the coming three days. Birds that long used to visit his balcony were nowhere around. They did not visit his balcony anymore; he had stopped keeping food and water for them.

Once he had a bougainvillea bush in his garden, where little sparrows, babblers, which fed on bees, would start chirruping at the break of dawn. They would fight with one another and hop from one branch to another branch in the safety of the thick and densely packed leaves, away from the evil eyes of kestrels and owls prowling for them. Before his wife's death he used to keep crumbled bread, a small amount of grain and water for birds daily in his balcony. He glanced at four nest boxes, all empty, nailed up on the wall and remembered how a carpenter had been called by his father to furnish a bed. He had flattered his father all day for those. He had promised his father to study hard and be obedient if he would order the carpenter to make those nest boxes. He remembered how he would look daily at them, sitting there for hours, watching for birds, spying at them. He waited eagerly for the slightest clue of a nest, keeping nesting material there for them, bringing dry grass from the playground of his school. He wouldn't let go anyone near them. You'll scare my birds, he would shout when the maid would come to wipe the floor. This guy is crazy, the maid would mumble and he would pretend he didn't hear. He was passionate about birds. It amazed him when he saw a sparrow entering in through the hole of the nest box to roost. There was no limit to his happiness when he had heard the amorous cries of the hatchlings in the box for the first time. He was so ecstatic to see the birds sharing their home with his own, the tiny family members of those little birds hopping around his house, perching on the bookshelf, filling the whole house with their calls. Their home pleased him.

He recalled a couple of days after his wife's death, how with a crestfallen countenance he had gone out to his garden. The bird's shrill chirping that day had annoyed him so much that he dug out the soil with a spade around the root of the bougainvillea bush, and uprooted it to throw over the wall. He then put up a ladder and climbed up to seal the entrance of all the nest boxes he had nailed up on the wall of his balcony.

He was reading the newspaper when someone knocked on the door. He knew who it was, his maid who was always in a hurry. Who else could knock on his door so desperately? Nobody else came to his place. He had stopped picking up the calls of his relatives, since the day his wife died due to cardiac arrest. He could visualize clearly in his mind the day he woke up early to leave for a meeting in Lucknow. He was supposed to take the morning train. He asked his wife not to make the breakfast. He knew she wasn't well. He had told her he would have something at the station, but she didn't budge and went into the kitchen before it struck four in the morning. He was still in his bathrobe when he saw his wife lying on the floor of the kitchen, unconscious, shivering terribly. He rushed to the hospital immediately, and was still on the way when she died. His only son, Bhaskar had come back from America after two days when the last rites were over, and left after staying only for a week. He said that he had some urgent work to complete there. Bhaskar lived in America with his American wife, and worked for a multinational company. He'd thought of asking his son to stay with him for a while, but when he saw them coming with their two huge suitcases trailing behind them, he didn't say anything. From that day he lived alone, lamented alone. He shared his grief with no one. His son would call him once in a month or sometimes even forgot to do that, but he didn't mind. He would never call his son.

There are no vegetables to cook, sir, his maid jolted him back to present. Narayan stood up and went to his kitchen and opened the refrigerator. It smelled of rotten vegetables, there was a rancid smell of leftovers kept there for too long. The kitchen was in a state of disarray with nothing in its place. There were cups of tea scattered in the sink. He saw stains of tea spilled on the kitchen floor. Her maid would cook anything left in the refrigerator. She never asked him before cooking. She wouldn't wash vegetables properly. Her food would always be either overcooked or undercooked, and after cooking she would cover it with a lid and run away reminding Narayan to eat later before leaving for work. After his wife's death he never had hot breakfast; he would serve himself later what his maid kept for him in the refrigerator. She would come early in the morning. He thought of looking for another maid several times, but Savitri seldom took leaves, and in spite of her poor cooking abilities she had this quality which exempted Narayan from taking the trouble of cooking on his own. Where a septuagenarian widow would go at this age to look for a job, he used to think, every time the idea of firing her crossed his mind.

Give me five minutes, I'll buy some vegetables from the shop, Narayan told Savitri. You have tea for the moment, he added.

When Narayan grabbed his umbrella hanging on a nail, he saw his son's umbrella hanging next to it, folded, with a square canopy, square aluminium shaft and square rubber finished handle, exactly as he wanted. Bhaskar was firm on getting that, no other umbrella but the square shaped one he wanted, which his friend had brought with him to school. Narayan had looked for it everywhere in the city, searched in every shop. Rashmi, his wife had advised him not to give in to child's every demand so easily, but seeing his child so restless perplexed him and he had bought one eventually.

Narayan went down the road to the vegetable vendor, whose shop was in the next street. When Bhaskar was a child, he would persistently insist that Narayan take him to the vendor, every time he had to go there. He would hold Narayan's index finger tightly, and Narayan would feel the soft grip of his little hand, his tiny fingers curled up over his index finger. He recalled when Bhaskar stood up for the first time, staggering and falling several times; it was magical to see him approaching on his tiny feet, when he stood stretching out his arms to embrace him. He felt very proud and elated as a father. During those imperceptible moments, he had never realised that one day he would miss the intimacies of their touch, lost in time. Before departing for America, Bhaskar had touched his feet, but the touch felt foreign to him. It wasn't the same as when he used to hold his hand and embrace him, it had changed with time like everything does.

When he returned and handled fresh vegetables to Savitri, she had already made daal, rice and bitter melon. "There was some bitter melon left in the freezer, I had forgotten to check that", she told Narayan while rushing out.

Narayan ate his cold breakfast alone, with a Videocon television set turned off in front of him; five chairs of the dinner table remained vacant, same as they stood for a long time after his wife's death. There was a time when his wife and son would constantly ask him to pass bowls full of daal and rajma and the variety of dishes his wife would cook, while arguing about whose turn it was to get hold of the remote. It was for those simple family moments that Narayan dreamt of. He thought of retiring early so that he could have his lunch together daily, not only on the weekends as he used to have then. He would tell everyone in his office that he would take VRS soon, that he was tired of working and wanted to spend his future time with his son and wife. He had been planning to take a trip to Europe with his family with the funds he would get after retirement.

He was still planning when his son got a prestigious job in Boston. Narayan wanted him to work in India, but finding his son very enthusiastic about working in a foreign country, he persuaded his heart and bid him farewell with a heavy heart. It was hard for him to see his son boarding a flight, going far, miles away from him. He didn't go to the airport as he didn't want to cry in front of his son, he didn't want to show him how weak he was. He wanted to cry in his privacy. Sometimes he would take his son's photo at night, his long hairs cascading down his neck, a flute in his hand, dressed as lord Krishna, and he would start sobbing when his wife would beg him to be strong, but the pangs of separation were too much for him. After a few years Bhaskar stopped picking up his parents' calls, phoning them after a couple of days apologizing and blaming the heavy work load, then one day he told them that he had married an American girl. Narayan saw his daughter-in-law's photo when Bhaskar mailed them one week after their wedding, giving the same excuse as always.

Narayan put on his white shirt and black pant, pulled on a half sweater his wife had knitted for him, and left for work, for the last time in his life. After his wife's death his office was the only place where he could feel his worth. It was in the office where he could forget his lonely life.

On the way to his office every time, he used to think, how hard he struggled to get this job. He recalled how he would study from morning till night taking only little tea breaks. His wife would make tea every time she saw him yawning. His father had insisted that he get married even before he was in a job, and would seize every opportunity to push him to get married. Narayan wanted to marry only after he could stand on his own, but he had to surrender eventually, tired with his father's constant nagging. In the beginning of his career he was very excited about his job and did his work diligently, but with time his interest faded. He would daydream about the Europe trip he would take with his family, he would remind his colleagues that he was not going to do this job for long and would soon take VRS. His boss would come every now and then to his seat to warn him about the mistakes he often made. Sometimes he would post letters to wrong addresses; sometimes he would pass a bill without checking it properly.

When he reached his office everyone congratulated him.

"So the day finally came for the Europe trip. We'll miss an efficient employee like you, Narayan," his boss said as he patted him on the back.

In the evening everyone gave a farewell speech and gifts. His boss dropped him home that night with all the gifts he received. Narayan's eyes were misty, and felt a little sad when his boss left. He had never thought in his life that retiring would be so painful, that he would feel depressed at the sight of his boss leaving him behind.

Next day he started dressing once again. He put on his white shirt and black pant; he knotted the tie up to his neck and put on his favorite suit. Bhaskar had called him the night before, just after he came back from his grand farewell. He was expecting Bhaskar to ask him to move in with them. But then he also thought of refusing him, telling him he was too old to shift home now. He would tell him that he could not adjust to American norms of living, and had already prepared himself to say that, but his son called up only to congratulate him on the successful and immaculate completion of his career. He advised him to keep Savitri. "Dad, you should talk to Savitri. Ask her if she can stay as a full-time caregiver. You will need someone now," he had said. Narayan just put down the phone. He could only say to his son that he would do that, "don't worry about me". This was the last thing he had said to his son.

Before entering his office, he noticed that when he had first joined his office the area around it had been deserted, and that the scenery had changed drastically with time. Tall buildings and skyscrapers had sprung into existence imperceptibly. Time had flown unnoticed in his life, changing everything beyond his imagination and control.

He went straight to his seat, sat there and started moving his fingers through the bunch of papers lying at his table. He asked the peon for a glass of water. This was his routine everyday as he entered the office. His colleagues were astounded to see him like that. When his boss saw him through the glass door of his chamber, he walked to his seat.

"Narayan, how come you are here? You're retired now. You should enjoy at home," his boss said.

Home! It was the only word that echoed in Narayan's mind. He got up from his seat, dropped to his knees and started sobbing. His boss grabbed him. "Narayan, are you okay?" he asked.

Narayan broke down suddenly. He kept repeating, "Sir, sir, please let me be here..." His mind wandered back to the place that he used to call home, something of which is no more there, and never will be.

THE SCARF

After months when Sukhbir opened his eyes he found himself in a hospital amidst numerous patients. He didn't know for how many days he had been there. He only remembered a flash of light that dazzled him to blindness, the earth trembling beneath his feet, and the unbearable heat that tried to roast him alive, but then he lost his consciousness.

He didn't know how and when he was brought to the hospital. He was in coma for several days. The nurses told him. The day he opened his eyes, the first thing that came to his distraught mind was his daughter and wife.

Where are they? Perhaps, in the same hospital, in the same ward with him, he thought, but he had no strength to speak. He tried to part his lips and utter one or two words but it seemed impossible to him, and the effort itself drained him so much that he fell asleep once again.

It was the month of March when this happened. The weather was pleasant and Sukhbir's daughter was excited for the coming festival Holi. Each evening after Sukhbir returned from work he stepped off his bike and parked it in the narrow gallery on the north side of his house. He then retired straight to his reading room and reclined in his arm chair to relax for a while. After a while, his daughter would rush to his room holding a tumbler of hot coffee gingerly in her tiny hands, which she enveloped in a piece of cloth. She would put down the tumbler on his reading table and watch him till he finished his coffee. This had been his daughter's routine since a week. Before a week, it was Sukhbir's wife who brought coffee to his room. When Sukhbir finished his coffee, his daughter would curl her lips and ask in a low voice, "Are you tired today, papa?" A faint smile would flicker on Sukhbir's lips. His daughter was very talkative and never remained at a loss for a remark. She convinced him to go to the nearby market and buy her a water gun for Holi. His daughter reminded him of his childhood days when the festival filled him with exuberance. He grew excited before a week, squirted colored water and giggled with his friends. But he didn't feel that anymore. Perhaps, the real charm was in those childhood days, not in the festival alone.

City was flanked by such vendors those days who sold different colors, caps, masks and water guns on each side of the road. He thought of getting the things but somehow couldn't go to the market till this very day. It was the day when suddenly a terrorist attack shocked the entire city.

There was a chain of fierce bombing that happened at different places. The attack claimed several innocent lives. It was as if the whole city was painted with blood before Holi. He had seen terrorist attacks happening all over the country on television before. But that was TV news. It was something outside his life. During those evenings, as he met his friends in the old tea shop this news remained the main topic of their debate. He had never thought that he too could be a victim of a terror attack some day. Fear of death is a peculiar thing; it only scares you when it happens to your own people. Everyone knows it is inevitable but nobody accepts this till one dies.

This was the first terrorist attack in a residential area. They had never done it this way before. It had always been at some busy place, in a clamorous market or amid a procession or inside temples or mosques. But this attack was more intense, and casualties had been unprecedented. He came to know about it from the nurses. Nurses were around him all the time. All were from the poor families who worked diligently day and night to pay the bills and probably for the education of their children. He wanted to ask them if they too lost their near ones but he couldn't gather enough courage. Only a few could be saved and his wife and daughter were not in that list.

"You were lucky to be brought here in time," said the doctor. Sukhbir couldn't see his face clearly. His eyes felt watery. He couldn't resolve the outline of anything around him; the doctor looked blurry to him. He reached out his face and tried to cup his cheeks. The doctor smiled and inclined towards him.

"Take a lot of rest. You'll be perfectly fine within a few days. You're improving rapidly," whispered the doctor into his ears.

He heard those two words 'perfectly fine' and they kept ringing in his ears. Was he ever going to be perfectly fine again? After losing everyone from his family? How was he going to live the rest of his life with such immense pain? Is there any medicine for this? He wanted to cry out loud. Come apart with the agony that kept hurting him incessantly. But he had no more strength left to cry his heart out.

He had suffered from burns all over his body and a severe injury to his head that made him feel dizzy all day. After coming back to consciousness, he realised that he had been there in the hospital for months. He didn't know for sometimes if all his limbs were safe and intact. He was being injected all over his body, both his hands and legs felt numb, and a pipe was inserted through his neck to feed him. His mouth was covered with an oxygen mask. There were narrow tubes fitted all along his body. He had seen his mother when she was in the hospital, trying to tug those irritating tubes. But he himself couldn't even feel those tubes. Tranquilizers had left him deadened. Earlier in his life, when he had seen his mother in such medical condition he always wondered how could she stay in a bed for months, but now when he himself was in the bed for such a long time even the idea of leaving that bed never came to his mind. He couldn't even think that. He couldn't think anything; his mind felt empty. A song kept playing in his mind all the time on a repeat mode. It was a Dhrupad he had heard last in a concert with his family. On the day of Shivaratri, there was a concert of Dhrupad near Assi ghat, and he had gone there with his wife and daughter. He went there every year but this was the first time he attended the concert with his family. There were a few bookstalls outside the building, and he had just begun to go through a book when his daughter tugged his Kurta and started pulling him to move forward. She was eager to see the concert but she got bored within half an hour and started pressing him to leave. His wife also felt suffocated due to the smoke rising from the incense sticks. A few men were smoking cigarettes in a corner. He was completely engrossed in a young boy's performance. It was wafting through the corners of his untouched heart, and he already knew that it was going to leave a lasting impression on him. But he had to leave early as his daughter was too impatient. After all she was too young to listen to a Dhrupad recital!

He had to leave the concert in the middle of the young boy's performance. He was upset that finding a listener leaving in the middle of the performance the singer would think ill of his art. He wanted to go to him so much. He wanted to tell him that it was a mind-blowing performance and he would love to listen to him sometime again. But another thing also came to his mind; he thought what if the complete recital of Dhrupad doesn't end in a good note? At least not as good as he thought the beginning was! The impression that a part leaves could be better than the complete one! Couldn't it be like that? Sometimes it's better to leave in between when the things are not yet finished, he thought to himself. Sometimes the end is not as good as the beginning.

He always thought about this while he was writing. He always felt that the stories he wrote were good and fluent in the beginning, and they built up nicely, but as it neared the end he rushed to finish it. It just spoiled the whole thing. He used to think, if only he could leave his stories unfinished, incomplete! But people won't think it to be sensible, reading an unfinished story!

However, don't we all have unfinished stories? We all leave it in the middle, in the hope that the next person would do his best to finish it but he also leaves it somewhere in between when the things are only half done. There's no finishing line in the real life. His daughter and wife left him, all of a sudden, when the things were not complete. Also, he knew that he too would have to leave suddenly, somewhere in the midst of unfinished works.

After several days he was discharged from the hospital. He had gone straight to his house. His heart kept pounding against his chest. Looking at the old house brought tears to his eyes. He had never thought, not even in the scariest dreams, that his house would look so dreadful one day.

His father had built this house. This was the house where his daughter had kissed his cheeks for the first time. This was the house where his mother had taught him the tricks of gardening, about planting a tree. This was the house where he had hung a nest box in the balcony, and a pair of sparrows made a family of their own.

There was nothing left in the house except the precious moments he had lived there. Torched faces of memories welcomed him. Everything had turned into ashes and there was debris all around him. Burned memories were piled up in every nook and corner.

His mother's gold chain with a locket of lord Shiva's photo that he had kept near his mother's photo as a memento was not there anymore. It was stolen. Some rescuer must have taken it. He saw the photos lined up on the wall. Nothing was visible in them. Walls had turned dark due to smoke. Everything was burned to ashes, even his daughter's photo.

He remembered, his daughter had begged him once to take her to a movie. He had agreed reluctantly. He was not much of a movie fan.

"Why should I see someone else's imagination on screen when I can do that on my own while reading? Watching movies harms your power of imagination," he would always say. But he had to agree because of his daughter.

He glanced at his wife doing her hair from the mirror, parting her hair to put sindoor and sticking a bindi to her forehead. He wanted to take a photo but he didn't have the camera at the moment.

They went to a movie hall in the cantonment area. He remained in the movie hall but kept thinking of other things. He waited for his daughter to get bored, and soon she began insisting him to leave. Even when he didn't like the movie at all, in fact, he hated it and remained busy with his phone, it peeved him to leave the theatre. He didn't like this habit of his daughter. But his wife soothed his anger.

"She's a child, not a grown up," she said.

They left the theatre within an hour. They had to walk back to their home as they couldn't find a taxi. Taxi drivers had called on a strike.

Suddenly, his daughter stopped in front of a shop. She started begging him to buy a scarf. He was not in one of his good moods and it only infuriated him more. He moved ahead and walked briskly across to the other side of the road.

"I'm not buying anything anymore," he said in a raised voice with a disapproving look.

But his daughter began crying. She was very emotional like her father. A drop of tear rolled down her cheeks. She turned red in face. "I want this scarf. I wouldn't go a step forward until I get this," she declared, clenching her teeth. It was a fight between two passionate people.

His wife too pleaded. He loved his daughter. He couldn't see her crying for long. He said sorry and bought the scarf. His daughter screeched in joy and kissed him on cheeks. She seldom cried unless she was badly hurt. She had deep emotions which rarely surfaced.

They went ahead with the scarf. It was a beautiful scarf of pink colour. It was hand woven and furry. She looked pretty wearing that. He remembered when he was a child how he had slept holding his new shoes all night. In the same way like her father, that night his daughter slept holding this scarf in her hands.

"Keep it in the cupboard. It's yours only. Take it back in the morning," her mother said, but she didn't leave it. She kept holding it near her heart while she slept. Sukhbir woke up well past midnight. He found his daughter in deep sleep and tried to slip the scarf from her hands but her grip was tight. He smiled at her, stroked her hair and kissed her eyes. This memory was fresh in his mind. And he dreaded to lose that. He kept recalling the whole scene so that he doesn't forget it.

After getting discharged from the hospital and visiting his scorched house, he slept over at his friend's till he could decide for his future. It was going to take a lot of time to start his life again. He had to be strong; he had no other option. Life goes on with its cruel intent.

For months a nightmare bothered him. It was the same dream daily. He saw his daughter in his dreams, grown up and beautiful. She had come on wonderfully: an independent, bold and educated woman.

But in this nightmare, he heard his daughter crying from a far distance. There was an earthquake, and he felt the earth trembling beneath his feet. He heard his daughter crying for help. He remained so perturbed that he couldn't decide in which direction to run. He ran frantically everywhere, in all the directions but couldn't trace her. He faltered and staggered and couldn't run as fast as he wanted.

And then he saw her lying on the ground just behind him, as if she was behind a curtain and suddenly emerged. A heavy branch of a huge tree had fallen over her one leg, and she was wailing in pain. She was trying to free herself vigorously but couldn't.

"This guy said he wanted to take me with him. He's a devil, father. Oh! See his devilish smile. I felt so terrible. Please save me from him," she yelled out, pointing in a direction.

He turned towards the direction she was pointing, and he saw a guy under the fallen tree. His smashed head was underneath a heavy branch and blood had oozed from all over his head. Blood had washed his face, but he could see his grinning mouth and yellowed teeth. There was no palpitation. He didn't even flutter.

"He's dead. Don't worry. He wouldn't harm you now. Dead people are better than the living ones," he told his daughter.

He tried to lift the branch but it was too heavy for him. He tried to grab his phone with his shaking hands and call a friend for help, but he didn't know where he exactly was. He wanted to tell his mind that he was in a nightmare, but his dizzy mind overcame his power to resolve. It was precisely at this point that he woke up sweating, every night. How broken he felt when he realized that he couldn't save her even in dreams. A man is as helpless in a dream as he is in real life.

"So do you have nothing left of your daughter and wife," I asked Sukhbir when he stopped speaking.

"I have one thing that I keep with myself always," he said and took out something from his pocket. It was the same pink scarf her daughter had bought. It looked brand new.

"How come it looks so new? Didn't it burn with everything else?" I asked him and realized it was quite insensitive of me to ask him that. I felt embarrassed but it was impossible to take my words back, so I waited for him to reply anyway. He turned his face and looked in the other direction. He remained silent for a few minutes.

"It was safe under a stone in that burned house," he said and then again he went silent. But I waited as I gathered he wanted to say something further.

"They couldn't burn my daughter's scarf, she kept it so close to her heart," he said with pride.

WEIGHT OF DEMISE

There has been a peculiar relation between me and my dreams. In my dreams, I meet people whom I can't ever meet in this world again. Often, I see my mother with a prayer bell in her hand. She used to wake me by ringing it. Other times, I see my grandfather, his numerous Kurtas, his thick rimmed glasses under which his eyes seem larger and protruding. I see his old radio set playing next to him, wrapped in an old leather coat. And now I am as old as my grandfather was when he died, eighty seven years old to be specific, like a ripe fruit which can drop from the branch of this life anytime.

My memories have faded with time but like a scene from a movie, memories flash in front of my eyes sometimes.

However, today I didn't see my mother or my grandfather; instead, I saw a pair of eyes. I didn't even know whose eyes those were. A pair of tiny, round and black shiny eyes full of pity and love. And I saw those chasing me down the road. It followed me as I kept falling down the road. The eyes didn't belong to any face. It just slithered on the ground and rolled down the road behind me.

After a while it stopped and glanced at me as if asking me for a refuge. I tried to stop myself from falling but couldn't. I was almost rolling down a hill now, and it felt impossible for me to stand somewhere or to hold onto something. The distance between us was increasing very fast but the eyes were not getting any smaller. They remained the same size, still glowing with the same intense love. And then, I saw a blurred face, with melting outlines, coming over me, asking me for some water.

"Don't remove your clothes, Baba? It's cold baba."

But I kept pushing the blanket off me. My skin was dying and any touch felt terribly painful. They covered my head with a large cap my wife had knitted for me years ago. And I was trying desperately to remove it.

I was trying to unbutton my shirt all the time. Anything within a touching distance suffocated me. I was listening to a few people sobbing around me. I knew I was going to die very soon. But death didn't seem to scare me.

They put a few drops of water in my mouth with the help of a dropper. I couldn't bring it down. I had no energy to gulp it down. It lingered in my mouth and kept choking me. I felt the corners of my mouth going dry. I wanted someone to wet my lips but my voice was already dead. I could hear people whispering around me.

"Is it getting mottled around Baba's nose? Blood is not reaching there. The tips of his fingers are becoming blue. See the blotches."

"We're going to turn you Baba." I heard someone saying.

And they lifted my legs a little by unbending it. It had nothing, no flesh, except the fragile bones that could crack with the slightest stroke. They felt heavier now, perhaps, with the weight of death. They held me with my waist and turned me over to the other side. I gasped a few breaths. I tried not to waste those. How impossible the simplest task 'breathing' seemed to me. I wanted to turn to the other side from the time immemorial. I didn't want to look more in those black tiny eyes but the eyes were on the other side too. Everything was almost the same on the other side: the same landscape, the same road. Those pair of eyes was still rolling down on the same road. I kept falling down and down with the immense weight and those peculiar eyes stood there, watching me intensely.

"Baba, Baba, no baba, please baba"

I heard their scream getting louder around me. Shrieking cries filled the surroundings. But I was falling down farther and farther as I slowly sunk to a place far more relaxing and calm.

And then, all of a sudden, I was lifted up high in the air and dropped in a village with a thud. I didn't feel any pain, though my head smashed on the ground and my skull opened. My bones cracked and from it came out a little boy around nine or ten years old. He seemed to be cheerful and full of energy.

It was the first time I was in my village with my father. We walked along a canal on an elevated narrow trail. On the other side of the elevated path laid a huge mango grove. My father told me he had come there after twenty long years. After walking for several minutes, we reached our ancestral house. My father turned the key in the heavy lock made up of copper which had acquired a tinge of green with time, and pushed open the rusted gate. The house looked dilapidated. I could see the wide open cracks snaking everywhere on the wall. We could feel the dampness in everything we touched and the moisture wafting around us. Flakes of plaster would fall on the ground off the wall with a thud. Termites had partially eaten everything made up of wood: the doors, the almirah, the window casing. A thin and intricate trail of mud had covered the door of the bathroom. There was a layer of algae growth on the floor and over the walls.

My father bought a long pipe and cleaned the house and the bathroom. It took him three days to properly arrange everything. He had to buy a bed, as the old bed in my room had decayed with time.

After a few days, one afternoon, when I was reading a children's magazine under the sun, a small puppy came near me and sat hunched up near my chair. I thought he would leave after sometime but he started following me everywhere and stayed within the premises. He was little brownish in color and had one of the tiniest tails and charmingly attentive small ears that pricked up even with the rustle of wind. He ran on his tiny legs and went off balance with every sweep of a wind.

He must have been a month old but looked smaller and malnourished. His black shiny eyes seemed alluring. He would wag his tail as if he knew us for years. He seemed too little to be alone. His mother had to be somewhere near, we thought, and kept the door ajar. But neither had he left nor anyone came looking for him. He was alone and most probably an orphan, perhaps, with no one in the world. My father tried to shoo him off, telling me that he would become too dependent, and wouldn't be able to feed himself later. But every time he was thrown out of the gate he came in running from the little space between the thin rods. Although we hadn't given him anything to eat, he came along as if he was our pet for a long time, and had come all the way with us from the city.

Somebody had to take a stand for him, and I declared that I was going to adopt him.

I, a small kid, friendless and a loner hoped to find a friend in him. My teachers used to write in my copy: Child doesn't make friends, plays alone and does the class work very slowly. My father had told me that it was a challenge for me to make friends. And so, I gave him a name "Tuffy" and fed him a packet of biscuits to befriend him. He followed me everywhere, to the village pond, to the market and even to the bathroom. He sat next to my chair as I would read under a guava tree. A flock of crows circled in the sky and cawed harshly. There was one lame crow which always came about, and a cat had given birth to five litters in the garage. There was a pair of owl perched on the branch of a Neem tree; they roosted there in the night, there were buffaloes wading in the pond and Tuffy would watch everything with me.

There were plenty of cut woods in a store room with high ceiling. Taking a heap of woods out my father would make fire early in the morning and Tuffy would curl up near it.

One cold night when I woke up I found Tuffy snuggled under my blanket.

"Tuffy come here," I would say and he would stand on his tiny feet, look up alarmingly and come running behind me. If any strange person would try to come near me he would bark his heart out. I felt like I own a bodyguard, the most loyal one.

"He is so attached to you. How will he survive once you leave?" my father asked me.

"So does this mean I shouldn't make friends?" I remarked and he laughed at me. I fed him with whatever I ate. He didn't eat his own food but remained much interested in what I was having and kept staring at it.

Tuffy grew bigger and healthier. He wasn't undersized or underweight anymore. In fifteen days he was strong enough to stand up to a harsh wind. But I was sure not to leave him behind.

"Can't we take him to the city, father?" I asked my father one day.

"And, who will feed him? You'll be in the school," my father said frowning.

I was a sensitive boy. Craftiness of adulthood had not touched me yet. The mere thought of leaving him alone reduced me to tears. I started crying, a few drops of tear began rolling down my cheeks. "I want to take him with me. I can't leave him alone here. He has no one, not even his mother," I wailed.

"Tuffy will come with us," my father said, wiping my tears. He was also very sensitive. It was impossible for him to bear his child's unhappiness.

And soon the vacation was over. Our bags were packed and Tuffy too was ready to move with us to the city.

We waited for the bus at the end of a narrow path that led to the main road. I saw a huge bus rattling down the road. I was excited to sit in the bus with Tuffy. I was curious to see his reaction when he would look out of the window, traveling for the first time in a bus. My heart was full of happiness. I can't tell if I ever felt such happiness again in my life.

But as we climbed the steps of the bus, the bus conductor stopped me from entering.

"Drop the dog kid. Stray dogs don't travel in this bus," said the bus conductor, frowning with a stern looking face. His moustache was touching his ears and he had a face as big as a jackfruit. His bushy eyebrows gave him a look of demon. He had only a few strands of hair over his head that he had combed very carefully. "But this is our pet dog. I wouldn't drop at any cost," I protested. But his demonic look made me weak. I started crying and shouting, "Father tell him Tuffy is our pet dog."

"Drop the dog out of this bus or get down," growled the giant looking man.

My father snatched Tuffy from my hands and threw him out of the bus. How could my own father do that? To watch my dad doing that made me immensely unhappy and unforgiving. I rebelled. I stretched my legs on the bus floor. Two people grabbed my hands tightly as I put in all my energy to free myself. "We wouldn't get a bus after this Srijan, try to understand. Good boys do not cry for a puppy. I would get you a puppy in the city," my father tried to console me.

But would he be happy if he gets another child in the place of his own son! My mind reasoned and tears flooded my eyes.

I was hell bent upon taking Tuffy along. I was crying relentlessly. How could I leave my only friend alone on the road!

I was still trying furiously to free my hands when the bus gained some speed. I ran to the rear end of the bus holding the back supports of the seats. As the bus driver changed the gear, I fell down on the floor and cut my lips, a drop of blood oozed from the corner of my mouth. But, I rose to my feet immediately. A secret source of energy had unleashed itself. My father was running behind me, trying to get hold of me but I ran to the rear window.

I saw from the large rear window of the bus, Tuffy running behind us with all the might his tiny legs could afford. He too didn't want to leave. He ran and ran, howling and barking, but gave up after a few meters. He stopped huffing there but his black shiny eyes kept following me for a long distance. Those eyes kept looking at me as if pleading me to save them. I kept looking at those tiny eyes helplessly as I departed, for the last time, never to return.

PITCH DARK

On the way to my school, two or three blocks down the street from my house where the road forked into two and went across a narrow alley, there, at the end of it was an old house. It had a gigantic door of yellow color and walls were high up to ten feet or more.

We used to go there only to pluck some guavas from the tree that was inside the premises but its branches, which borne plenty of fruits, stretched out to the street. We would run to the house and begin pelting little stones aiming the branches. Ring neck parrots, dark crows and red whiskered Bulbuls were also its beneficiaries and they reached the top before our stones could reach.

An old woman used to sit there at the steps of the house. She would point out the ripe fruits to us. In the beginning, we all were afraid of her, thinking she was the doorkeeper. Her wrinkled white cotton sari looked as old as she was. We always thought that the stick she had in her hands was to shoo us off. But she was a lovely woman who loved children and it was her grandchild's house.

My mother told me she was Ratan's maternal grandmother. Ratan's mother was the only child she had and when Ratan's parents died in a car accident, she sold her house along with all the estate and came to live with the young lad.

She became a widow years ago when she was just thirty years old. She lived alone ever since. All her life she had kept herself busy caring for Ratan's mother. But, after she married her off, she was left with nothing to do.

After Ratan's parents' death she decided that it would be good for both of them to live together. Whatever money she got from selling the house and land she deposited it all in a bank, and from the interest bore all the expenses of house and Ratan's education.

However, Ratan grew up to become an alcoholic. In the beginning, he drank secretly but as the old lady's strength deteriorated and old age descended on her and the time he was on his own, he quit his school and began drinking at home in front of her.

Soon, I became fond of the old lady and started visiting her on holidays. She would keep some fruits separate and wait there at the steps for me. She would always be there on the steps as if this was the only part of the house she owned. I rarely saw her going inside. She would wave at every neighbor passing by to come over and chat. She would ask about the wellbeing of every person she knew in the neighborhood as if they were her family.

Every few weeks, she would give me delicious, spicy pickles of different fruits. It soon became her hobby to pickle every possible fruit. However, I loved the pickles of freshly cut radishes more that she grew in her garden. I found that mouth watering. I was not a glutton but her pickles revealed my appetite for good food.

My mother told me that Ratan was a scoundrel; he often tortured the old lady. She told me that he threatened to kill her whenever she opposed to his drinking. Once, in a rage, he threw her out of the house and refused to let her in. People said that she had to stay in the neighbor's house for a week, but she was so sentimental that she always remained worried for Ratan and even after all that she begged him to let her stay together. However, since that incident happened she would cook for him only when it was really needed. He lived on the upper floor, and she in a small room on the ground floor where she used to go in only after dusk.

Ratan did nothing all day, and drank so much that soon he was bankrupt, and it became hard to pay even the bills. He would quarrel with the old lady for money that he suspected she had kept safe from him. He had run up huge bills in every nearby shop. He wouldn't let her turn on the lights after the sunset. He complained that he could not pay electricity bills. She had to spend her evenings in the dark. I came to know about this, when one night I went to her house. It was a hot sweltering night, and my mother sent me out to her house to give her a hand fan she had bought especially for her. When I went there it was dark in her room, and she was lying in her bed. There was not a single window in the room. I felt suffocated cooped up within those four walls submerged in the darkness. Ratan had cut the electricity supply for her room.

"Why did you come at this time, it's so dark and hot, you see," she implored in a shaking voice, sitting by the bed.

"Dadi, don't you have power supply in your house," I ventured to ask her, fearing it might upset her.

"O child! We have, but we are going through hard times these days. Ratan doesn't have much money to pay the bills. You should have come in the daytime," she said, shaking her head.

I gathered that she was in a stupor of high fever as she touched my hands.

Since then I never went there after the sunset. It looked like a haunted house. Pitch dark inside the entire ground floor. He had not given her even a lantern. Upstairs one could see a dim light flickering timidly where Ratan drank alone.

After a few years I had to leave my home town to study in a college miles away. I missed my house too much there. The comfort of home was nowhere to be found. I was a sort of recluse, and I liked my privacy, but there I had to share my room with two other students who smoked and drank and forced me to take a sip. I would refuse them humbly and go up to the roof of the hostel from where I could see the green tops of many trees. There were trees with mango, guava and pear, and bushes of pomegranate and lemon, and I would start feeling homesick. My heart longed for my home, for my village day in and day out.

I missed the green pond where I jumped in and took bath for hours. I missed the guava tree. I missed the homemade food. I remember I couldn't eat much for weeks. The spicy food took toll on my appetite. I ate a little only on Wednesday when they made curry of spinach. I used to count my days there. I still remember how I had hung a calendar and crossed every passing day on it. My college was miles away from the city. My heart craved to see a family there. Whenever I saw an old lady I felt sad remembering Ratan's grandmother.

I would miss the pickles old lady gave me. Her delicate skin, her trembling hands marked all over with blue protruding veins, her white cotton sari, and her slightly tilted head. I missed everything about her. On weekends I went to the town to watch movies. But the town wasn't as homely as my village. I was in a town where nobody knew anybody and talking to strangers was thought to be crazy. Roads, parks and temples were swarmed by people; population was growing at an alarming rate but the houses were empty with the shrinking families. Loneliness was thriving there under the guise of crowd.

My heart pained, and I was anxious to come back to my old place, to my mother, to the old lady, to the guava tree, to the narrow streets, to the full-fledged joint-family, to back to love.

And soon the time came, I remember as I kept noting down the passing hours on my table. It should be still there but I think only a homesick boy would come to understand that. It was just the numbers in descending order that I wrote on the table, but to me it was coming close to my life. I had already packed my bag in the morning. I decided not to go back to the hostel and hired a taxi instead just after the class.

I reached the platform two hours before the train arrived. My friends laughed at me, "Grow up, have some snacks and then leave. Train might not have arrived yet," they had said. But I didn't hear them, I was better a child, I thought.

As the train arrived at my home town late in that freezing night, I alighted and walked out of the station. Hardly had I set foot in the town when I saw my father. He was in his old shabby khaddar jacket; his maroon muffler was wrapped around his throat. He was waiting for me already there.

We traveled home on his old Bajaj scooter that rattled through the meandering roads. Cold frigid wind was blowing across my face. A thick blanket of fog had covered the whole city, the dim yellowish sodium vapor lights of street sodium lamps flickered down at us, and dogs barked at us. How much I loved those dogs! At least they barked at me; at least they seemed to recognize me!

Next day, as soon as the sun was coming up, I set out to meet the old lady but she was not there on the steps; guava tree was drooping. I tried to push the door open but I noticed an old rusted lock hanging there.

I ran to my mother and asked her for their whereabouts.

My mother collected her thoughts and this is what she told me:

"The old lady died one dark night after a few months you left. She had come to our place once in her white cotton sari asking for you. There was a jar of juicy, spicy pickles in her hands; but when I told her that you left for college and would come after months she looked crestfallen. You took her passion away from her, snatched away her days, I guess. Guava tree withered and birds flew away within months after the old lady died. She used to water all those plants and trees.

Ratan sold her jewelry which she had kept safe in the bank locker, and hired a young lady to cook for him. There was a rumor that he was smitten with her and started selling everything in the house to buy her sari and other things.

One day, Ratan tumbled down the stairs and broke both his legs. He had to spend his last days in the same bed the old lady had died. People said, the young lady he had hired blackmailed him for money. She didn't give him much to eat during his last days when he was totally helpless. Some people suspected that it wasn't a natural death; probably she had poisoned him. Nobody knows when he died. There was a rumor in the neighborhood that he had died days before people came to know. Children were afraid to enter that narrow alley anymore; they said there a ghost screamed at night: "it is so dark here; it is so pitch dark in here." But soon, after the death of Ratan the voice was heard no more.

And although, it resembled a ghost's voice, I was pretty sure it wasn't a ghost, but it was Ratan's voice screaming out of endless darkness.

INCOMMUNICADO

All my life I looked for a friend. I was born deaf and couldn't speak the language everyone spoke. One learns the language by hearing it from others. It always remained complicated, as I wasn't very sure that I couldn't speak; I tried but in vain. I chose not to speak at all later. I knew people wouldn't understand me. My brothers could speak very well and so eventually no one was bothered anymore about me. Where in this talkative world would I have looked for a silent friend?

When I was only a year and a half, my grandmother insisted that I should be taken to a sorcerer. She was convinced that I was seized by an evil spirit. The news got spread in the neighborhood like wildfire and brought me humiliation. People love doing that. They always look for something to make fun of.

It made me so nervous that I refused to go out at any cost. I just disappointed my parents by staying at home all the time. Children mocked me even when they just saw my shadow out of home. It was better for me to stay at home than to face the abuse. Children jeered at me as if I was an alien. They forced me to live like an alien.

My parents had taken me to a fair once. They had to go through a lot of trouble when I got lost in the crowd.

The trauma of being lost and not being able to say anything remained with me all my life thereafter. Being mute was exactly the same.

I remember that dark night clearly. I was frantically looking everywhere but couldn't locate my parents. There were strange laughing faces all around me as though they were laughing at my pitiful state. Roads were dimly lit with red decorative lights. Roadsides were flanked by toy sellers.

I kept moving forward, dragged by some unknown force, looking everywhere but not being able to focus on one face.

Then out of nowhere, I saw two huge faces, bathed in red light, approaching me. They looked like giants in size, perhaps, because I was so terrified with the gloom of the place. It was full of people but I was carrying my gloom along. I saw their lips parting; they made gestures, trying to get something out of me but I just cried helplessly.

They too got tired of me like my parents. They dropped me at the help center, asked me to sit on a table and left. My parents found me an hour later or so, but from that day I sank deeper and deeper into my melancholic self. Although I was wrong at that time, but I felt as if my parents didn't try much to find me soon. It's always hard for a sad person to trust people.

Why do people with speech disabilities should have friends from the same flock! The thought had come to me when I had seen two mute friends once. My parents were taking me to a doctor. I saw them talking with each other in signs, making different gestures, sharing a laugh. However, finding a true friend has remained the never dying dilemma even for people who could speak and hear quite fairly, it has indubitably been the biggest failures of the civilization. We developed a language so articulate yet we always have to look for the right words to convey our true emotions. But words are so inefficient. No word, I think, has ever past anyone's lips that completely relieved and contented one's heart. Tears do better than words sometimes.

Sometimes, following my stubborn heart I took initiative and tried to communicate to people who could talk, but I badly failed. Children from my neighborhood never took me as a normal child. They never accepted me and I never understood them, except one thing, that I became a laughing stock for them each time I tried to open my mouth. I never felt abnormal though; I could share my emotions fairly well as anyone could do; only my ways were different. They took my muteness as an illness. And I was bound to grow up without any friend.

When I was around thirty years old my parents got me married to a girl from a remote village. She could speak and hear. Yes, I wanted to get married as I anticipated a friend in my wife. I thought the search for a friend would be over but now. But unfortunately we lived in two different worlds. Two separate worlds which never touched each other. I regretted marrying her, she wasn't happy with me; although, it wasn't my fault alone. She was ashamed of marrying me: a deaf and mute person and she never really accepted me. I think she never told her friends about me. She feared the social disgrace that could have brought to her with my introduction. I was a social disgrace, an embarrassment for her. We were so different that we didn't even care about sorting out the differences. The biggest and the most terrible difference was that I was willing to give it a chance but she was reluctant.

She belonged to a very poor family and it was the only reason her parents married her to me. But soon after the marriage, she made her own separate world in the kitchen. She spent all her days there and I kept myself locked in my room. In the beginning, she was disinterested but later I think she started taking pity on me. Our relation was more like the relation between a beggar and a passer-by who donates him a penny daily. She served me food the same way. I don't remember the time when we had looked into each other's eyes for more than ten seconds. There were hardly any such moments. We never even fought with each other. Such circumstances never occurred to our life. Our relationship lacked any such intimacy. The marriage wasn't even a failure; it was in the real sense dead. There was nothing to argue for. I wasn't very sure that whether in stark daylight, if we had come across each other on the road, out of our home, we would be able to recognize each other or not! But she made another world out of her kitchen, and it was her praying room where she prayed for hours. And I was quite sure that I remained in her prayers. It was the only place where she recognized me; the only place where I existed for her. This was the only bonding we had.

I was living in an isolated atmosphere where nobody could enter but she wasn't so lonely. She had made friends with neighbors and tenants who lived in the ground floor. She was a completely different personality with me. We didn't have many expectations from each other but sometimes it made me feel sad that never in our married life we shared a laugh or any grief. To say that I never expected anything from her would be a lie.

I continued to live without any friend but it started to change after she came into my life. According to my wife, she was just an accident, a terrible accident. But this accident didn't kill anyone, in fact, it brought life to a dead man, whose heart had stopped beating long before. She gave voice to my mute heart. Her smiles made my world brighter. She was dressed in red, green, blue, yellow, as to give my world a new color each day. Before she appeared, I felt like I was dropped in a running washing machine, caught in its whirl. And I kept whirling round and round until she came into my life, turned it off and rescued me out. She was my daughter, who looked exactly like me. There was this striking resemblance in the looks and in the traits. She had exactly the same features, the same lips, the same nose, the same eyes, even the same crooked smile. Sometimes in the past, while swimming in the ocean of my wild imaginations I had wondered how would I have been if I were born a girl and she was gifted to me by God, perhaps, to answer this.

I remember how fearful I was about her for a few months after her birth. I didn't even dare to check if she could hear or not, not until she was five months old. I would clap in all the directions and would eagerly wait for her to turn her face. I didn't want her to live without any friend like me. I didn't want her to face the same abuses I had faced. She wasn't deaf or mute, fortunately.

When I would take her out to the park or to the street, the things that attracted me caught her attention too. I felt that the search for a friend was finally over and so it was. As she grew up she started accompanying me on my occasional walks to the Ghats. I was afraid that like her friends from the school or neighborhood she would also start liking the ugly shows on television or going to the malls and partying, and I would be alone for once and all again. But from the very young age she liked peaceful places and the slowness of life. Like me she had a penchant for nature and she could hear it. I never had to teach her anything. She knew me as if she lived under my skin. How complete silence felt with her! With her, even signs seemed futile and silence seemed more articulate. Now, when I remember those days I feel as if they were the shortest days of my life, but those were the only days that filled up my memories to the brim. How much love a human being possesses! What an immense world of emotions resides in us. We are, after all, our own limitless universe.

On some sunny days, when the weather would be pleasant, me and my daughter would take out our cycles, and go out of the city in search of a pond; where we saw children bathing and jumping from the branch of the tree into the water. It cherished both of us to see the children playing in the water. I was deaf but my heart could hear the giggles. My daughter brought those giggles in my life. It was our therapy in the long summer afternoon. I didn't know how to swim but my daughter knew. She had learnt swimming in the school and she taught me later. And we jumped into the pond together.

It wasn't just a pond, it was an ocean of happiness and we swam in it together.

She had some friends from her school. She wasn't like me only. I had seen her joking with her friends, loosing herself free. Of course, she had some part of my wife too. Beyond my world she was like her mother, between us a bridge and for our marriage she was the life support.

We together looked for the meadows on the weekends. In the crowded city we found places where nobody was around. We looked for such open places. I remember when we would lie down on the stretched out carpet of grass, and we would stare at the sky, vast blue sky without the slightest hint of clouds, without a single bite, it felt like we owned the world. My heart was filled with happiness. I didn't need anything else except the never tiring comfort of silence between us. Daughters are the best friends, I realized.

My daughter used to play violin. She would play in front of me and I liked watching her play. I never got bored of it. I could feel the music.

One cold wintry night, my wife passed away peacefully. We came to know only in the morning when she didn't wake up. Nothing went upside down, not much changed. I saw my daughter crying and only when I wiped my face I gathered that I was crying too. I was sad for my daughter and for the man who lived in her prayers, because, I saw the man from her prayers disappearing with her. I didn't need that wretched man anymore though. It was true that I was tired of being in her prayers but I loved her. She did her best for me. She departed with her universe. And I wondered, if in a few coming years someone would even remember that such universe existed once. How selfishly private we are! Each one has a sun and a moon of one's own. I remember, I rested my forehead at her feet and cried to the contentment of my heart. She didn't have much space in my life but after her death I could feel the vacuum. Every dying person creates a vacuum and this world is full of vacuum space, I think, where gloom rests. Why do we feel gloomy for no reason? Do we enter the vacuum sometimes?

My daughter didn't go out for weeks after my wife's death. And a few months later, she got an invitation from a foreign University for a research project. But she refused to go. Instead she joined a software company. I felt guilty that I was the reason. It was me holding her back and I tried to persuade her, insisted her many times but she didn't agree.

Right at that time a memory flashed in my mind. It was when she was only five months old and I was walking on the roof. My arms were wrapped around her and I felt tired walking up and down. I came downstairs and put her into her mother's lap. I didn't even turn to see if she was crying or wanted to be with me. I just left. When she was brought to me again after a few hours, she smiled so cheerfully that I just hated myself for keeping her away for so long. I felt like I betrayed her. What if, after returning from abroad, she smiles in the same way again? What if her watery eyes had the same twinkle? Wouldn't it break my heart? I didn't press her to pursue her PhD again. But still, I knew my daughter wouldn't live with me forever. I knew one day she had to move on. One day she would leave the nest and take a flight. I couldn't keep her in a shell forever.

I remember when she was only six months old I used to put up the bedcover like a tent to make a house for both of us. All of a sudden the outside world would disappear leaving only two of us together. She loved being with me under the roof of that bedcover. She felt safe. She smiled. I could still visualize her smile. She would screech with joy. But then I couldn't keep her under it forever. It was the time again when the world will come into her sight. I wanted her to marry and make a family and a carrier of her own.

And, not after long the day came. She told me about the boy from work she was in love with. She wanted to marry him. I had full trust on her choice. He had an offer to work in a multinational company in California. My daughter wanted him to work here so that she could come to me on weekends. But things cannot always be the way you want.

Soon after the wedding they had to take a flight to America. I was sad and happy at the same time. I was finally freeing her but to see my only friend leaving saddened me. She told me through signs that she would come back very soon, that she wasn't going forever. But I sobbed like a child. We sobbed together at the airport. That day I wanted to say so much to her. That day, I felt as helpless as I did when once I got lost in a fair. My inability to speak felt like an illness once again. First time in my life she too wanted to say a lot and I think she whispered something into my ears. I think she said something which filled my heart for the lifetime and gave me power to live further. I think she said that with me she never looked for a friend.

After she was gone I began to make a terrace garden. I bought a few pots and arranged those on the roof. I planted flowers. I planted my daughter's favorite plants. I missed her but I wasn't very sad. I had learnt to occupy myself. She had already taught me talking with silence.

A few years went past when my daughter came back with a new little friend. I felt elated to see my granddaughter. Now I had two friends. She would read poems to me which she had learnt in school.

I know my son-in-law must have thought it foolish of his daughter reading in front of a deaf old man. But he will never know that my deaf ears heard her poems and I hummed along with it.

TOY SELLER

I was new in the city; a complete stranger knowing no one there. I had no friends there in the strange city and out of boredom I would go out alone and walk around the park area. However, I would seldom enter the park, detesting the noisy crowd over there. I preferred solitary walks, avoiding any eye contact, enjoying my solitude.

However, on some days, I would go to the park, just for a change, and would lean back in a chair after brushing the dust off it. I would have my little book with me, the one I had read several times and yet wasn't bored of.

One evening, I had just started reading when a little boy came near me. He was around ten years old, and was holding the strained strings of colourful gas balloons in one hand. A long stick was inclined to his left shoulder and a few toys were tucked to it. His hair was dirty and unkempt. His discolored shirt stopped above his waist and cuffs were rolled back as the shirt was smaller than his size. His pants were loose on his waist as it was lacking a button. It was tied with the help of a rope; it was the first thing I had noticed. He started pleading with me to buy his toys. I told him that I didn't want a toy but he kept insisting and out of pity I had to buy one. I had no need of toys then. I didn't have any children.

I had come there for a change and to forget the excruciating pain I had felt when a nurse showed me the dead body of my newborn child, our first baby. The agony was unbearable. I was so distressed to see him; his eyes were tightly closed and swollen; his eyelids were not visible. Never in my dreams had I thought of such an experience. It couldn't happen to me, I wasn't a bad person. I had heard my parents say many a times 'you reap what you sow'. I hadn't done any wrong to anyone. I wasn't the rigid one. I hardly argued with anyone over any issue, not unless it harmed someone. My wife detested my timidity and diffidence. Perhaps, the ways of fate are beyond questioning.

I was so excited to see my child for the first time. My wife would take my hands and put it on her belly to make me feel its kicks and movements. I would dream of my child's first cry into this world. But when the nurse brought my baby, he was cold, silent, and he never cried. He looked exactly like my wife, looking as stubborn as she is, determined not to open his eyes to this world ever. Doctor asked me to give this news to my wife as she believed only I could keep my wife calm. I collected myself but my tears were irresistible and they kept rolling down to my cheeks, washing down my face. When I told my wife that our baby was born dead, that his umbilical cord was entangled to his neck, she looked straight into my eyes with her impenetrable gaze and a frozen face, and I knew that she wasn't looking at me. She had lost herself and like my child she too didn't cry thereafter. She became as silent as a stone. Psychiatrist suggested that we should change our environment a bit, and that's when I decided to come to Varanasi. In the beginning, I wanted to go to some quiet place, aware about the hustle and bustle of the oldest city, but my friends suggested that the experience would rejuvenate me. Didn't we already have too much silence in our lives, I thought.

It was a single room apartment with an attached toilet, somewhere in the labyrinth of old crooked streets near the river. We lived on the second floor, and through the small rusted window I could see the placid river flowing , unaware of our troubles and trauma. I wondered, if I could ever be like the river. No matter what happened to its fate it remained the same, calm and composed. There were red faced macaque monkeys everywhere. One would come to my window ledge, hopping from one building to another. He would sit there for hours and keep begging for some food. It kept me entertained for a while, but it was impossible to throw those few bitter moments out of my life.

I remember, after my mother's death, I had asked my friend how many years did it take him to forget his father's death completely. He told me, only a few months. But, my mother's death did change my life totally. I could never become the same person I was at the time my mother was alive. I wonder if people we love take away some part of our own lives along with them when they die. I knew I wouldn't ever forget my child's death too. I knew I had lost some part of my life as he departed.

I'd come to Varanasi to get away from people, but from that day it became a habit going to that park, and meeting Rahul daily in the evening. After cooking, feeding my wife, doing the dishes and finishing the daily scores I would go there to sit at the same corner, and would find him already perched there, dangling his feet, waiting for me. I'd hired a caretaker for my wife. I would buy a few toys daily from Rahul; I couldn't tell why exactly, perhaps because I felt pity for him or for the child I thought I would father in the future. I would hide those so that my wife shouldn't see them. I would buy a bottle of juice daily for Rahul and he would drink it off in no time. He would wipe his mouth with the back of his hand as his shirt was too dirty.

Rahul would always be gleeful. He would tell me jokes and would laugh out loud himself on those. His thin body trembled when he giggled boisterously. I wondered if my child would have laughed the same way. Rahul would cough frequently while talking. His fragile body had an effervescent spirit. I didn't find his jokes very amusing but, when I would see him laughing merrily it gave me a chuckle too, and I couldn't resist laughing. This is the best part of laughter, only if people knew that, it's contagious! As long as I remained with him everything felt happy and vibrant as his unrestrained laughter disseminated vitality across the park.

Sometimes, he talked about his family. He told me that his father was an alcoholic and mother was a sweeper. He told me how his father beat his mother daily. He beat him also if he couldn't sell enough toys. He would call his father a monster. He dreaded if one day he would kill both, him and his mother. I remember, he asked me once if I drank. I had seen his watery eyes then. I can still visualize those asking eyes eager to hear from me an intense 'No.' Perhaps, God made lies for this: to bring happiness in a child's life, to comfort a child, to bring smile and contentment on one's face. Perhaps, humans have misinterpreted each and everything.

Autumn arrived. Afternoons seemed golden as if a little of gold was blended in the air. Sky was blue as a vast ocean. There was chill in the air. Rahul's cough became more frequent. I tried to give him some money but he refused to accept. He dreaded that if he accepted money, his mother would suspect him of stealing. He didn't want to become a thief in his mother's eyes. He was a hero for his mother, her only hope, her only heroic dream.

He would always be in his tattered sweater. But his sweater wasn't sad of its state just like him. He told me, once he had asked his father for a new red sweater as it was his birthday, and his father had run behind him with a bamboo stick. But he was so drunk that he was staggering and couldn't chase him down. He told me that he had laughed too much when he saw his father falling in the gutter which was running beside the narrow lane. He asked me if it was wrong to laugh as his mother had shouted at him, got angry that he should rather have helped him. But, I told him it's wrong to suppress laughter. I told him that laughing is exactly the same as worshipping. I knew he wouldn't understand, but he laughed.

My wife's health improved a little. She started to talk, though in a feeble voice. We would go together to the bank of river Ganges and sit there for a while, looking at the serenity of the placid river that flowed deep and steady, inflicting upon us the meditative disposition. My regular meetings with Rahul came to a halt as my wife requested me not to go out and rather stay with her. I'd started to love the place but holidays were coming to an end.

I had to leave Varanasi the next day on an early morning train. A day before leaving Varanasi, my wife had told me that she wouldn't ever be able to conceive again. I was shattered. My wife told me that she had gone through some tests while I was out. I could see her welled up eyes while her quivering lips said those words. They trembled on her lips for a while before coming out, with difficulty. She thrust reports in my hands. It was a disaster imposed upon us but we accepted our fate. If something is inevitable it's better to welcome it with stretched out hands, I thought. We hugged each other tightly and cried together for hours to console ourselves. Perhaps, it was the only way to heal our wounds.

I went to meet Rahul one last time. I gathered that there was not much I could do. We both were bound by our destinies. We both were doomed. I returned him all the toys I had bought from him. I didn't want my wife to see all those toys, and after all they were of no use now. I returned it all to Rahul knowing beforehand that he too wouldn't keep those with him, and would sell those eventually. At an age when other children played with toys, his cruel fate made him sell those.

Alas! Possessing a toy was not in our fate.

However, Rahul was smiling the last time I saw him; his powerful soul was determined to fight back his brutal fate.

I had gifted him a red sweater and he was still staring at it with his amazed eyes when I turned around to leave. He had only learnt about earning daily to survive. A gift from a stranger was beyond his imagination.

There were no signs of miseries on his face. He seemed like the richest man on the earth right then.

But he was like this always, with or without a red sweater. He was like that happy, serene, ever flowing river, I always wanted to be.

SURREAL LIFE

That day I was feeling too hot. I could feel the beads of perspiration on my forehead. My body was drenched with sweat. It was a sweltering afternoon. I was looking for a hand fan and I could see that resting on my writing table but it seemed impossible for me to reach there. My legs felt numb and weak. My knee felt unable to carry my body's weight. I felt lethargic as if I had run for many miles and had finally drained and collapsed on the ground. I tried to stand on my feet but I felt somebody had put an immense weight on my chest and was stopping me even to raise my limbs. I tried to free myself and throw my limbs in the air like an infant but I felt I had been tied to something. I wanted to shout but I felt choked and there was no one around except the immense blurred space. I could not exactly gather where I was, the surrounding seemed incomprehensible but I could hear the distant sound of some construction vehicles. I could not see them, but it was as noisy as a bulldozer, excavator or a cement mixer.

After a while I heard a door open and there she was, my grandmother. She looked older than her age when she died. I could see her face clearly, although everything else looked blurred, but she was as clear as fresh water. One of her pale eyes had cataract. I could see the cloudiness in the lens of her left eye. Her hair was long, free, thick and disheveled. She cast me a smile, revealing her bare gums, not a single tooth was there in her mouth. On the back of her hand there were several protruding veins, and a green tattoo, some obscure sign, she had told me, she had got it painted long back in her childhood. I could see her wrinkled face. I had never seen so many wrinkles in one face before. She never looked this old, but then it looked like she had come straight out of her deathbed and of course it had to be so, because it couldn't be an illusion, I remembered clearly, she died many years ago. I was flabbergasted to see her again. How could it be possible? I still remember the morning when she passed away. And there I was seeing her again after so many years. A strange fear besieged me. I wanted to yell but nothing came out of my mouth, it was like I had lost my ability to talk. I was profusely sweating as she was slowly approaching me. And then I saw my wife coming through the door and she saw my grandmother but she wasn't astonished. It seemed normal to her to see a dead woman standing there. I wanted my wife to take me out, but there was a pleasant smile on her face.

"See, grandmother is here to see you", she said smiling.

"I'll be here only for two months, only for two months, not one day more, not one day less," she cried.

She started crying loudly. My wife tried to console her but she kept crying.

Only two months, only two months, she kept repeating, and it was then that my dream busted and I woke up. I swept a glance all over the place, I tried to resolve my surroundings, and there I found my little daughter sleeping next to me. There was a heavy quilt over my body, and I was drenched with sweat. I got out of bed with difficulty as my knees felt jammed. My room was filled with the commotion sound of washing machine. My wife was there in front of me.

"You slept like a log, you never slept like this before in the noon," she said.

"Baby was crying relentlessly, she has high fever. When will you take her to the doctor?" She asked, "Her health is deteriorating day by day, I think we should change the medication."

I splashed some water on my face, and then I told my wife that I would take baby to a new doctor in the evening, wiping my face with a ragged towel.

I went downstairs, dragged my bike out of the gate and raced towards the Ghat.

But I could still repeat that dream. My grandmother's smiling face was still fresh in my mind. I could still hear her cries. Only two months, only two months, it was still echoing in my head. There was heavy traffic on the road, and in front of me people were squeezing out from the narrow roads, dragging their bike up to the pavement, trying hard to find some space to get through. But I was still somewhere else; perhaps I was still in my dream.

I reached my friend's house, and called out to him. He lived in a big old house with three courtyards where many cats would freely roam about. One cat came near my feet and started brushing it. The cat too looked as if out of a dream. I could see the mischievous glint in her eye, as if she too was trying to manipulate me. The cat looked brooding. She kept scratching herself at my feet. She purred mournfully. I wanted to kick the cat out of my way as she looked terrible and ominous but she clung to my legs and curled herself.

My friend was a tenant there and his landlords lived abroad. The house was so old that flakes of cement would come down with a thud every now and then. From one courtyard you could see the branches of a huge peepal tree that had grown from one of the surrounding walls of another courtyard; its roots had run down the wall to the ground and had clung to everything that came on its way.

I was still looking at the gigantic tree when my friend came out of his room and we walked down slowly out of the main gate and passed through the narrow alleys to widely open Ghats. We didn't say a word to each other, it was our routine to go there together and watch the placidly flowing river for hours while sipping lemon tea.

There were not many faces around that day on the river bank, only a foreigner girl wrapped in a woolen shawl who was sitting, sipping her tea. Someone was playing a flute, although I couldn't see him but a distant melodious sound was wafting through the air. However, I was still puzzled, I was still pondering over my dream.

It was a dream of course, it could happen only in a dream, I thought. She had died long back and I could still remember that day.

It was a cold morning and mist had covered the whole city. You couldn't see farther than two meters. I was still in my bed under a thick blanket, and my wife was snoring next to me when my father's phone rang. He was in the other room. I didn't sleep a wink and I heard the phone ringing twice. My father was in deep sleep as he didn't pick up the phone. When I got out of my bed the phone started ringing for the third time. I went to his room and tried to push the door open but it was locked, and I was about to knock when my father picked the phone. I heard him talking behind the door. I could comprehend nothing from there and then my father's raspy voice went silent, and I saw the door opening and my father emerging from his room, rubbing his misty eyes. "Your grandmother passed away", he told me. She lived with my uncle across the road in an old house which my grandfather had built in the late fifties. In the beginning we all lived together harmoniously but after few years things changed and familial discordance became irrevocable. My father bought another house in the same colony.

I woke up my wife and gave her the news, but it didn't affect my wife much. We all went to my grandfather's house. She was lying down on the ground and my uncle was putting some water in her stiff mouth. Her mouth was wide open as if she was amazed by her own death. I heard people talking around me that her poor soul left her body through her mouth. Her eyes were half shut and her body was as cold as ice. Her thin skin seemed stuck to her bones, as if she had been vacuumed from inside by a Hoover, and only an immense hollow was left inside. I saw my octogenarian grandfather weeping in a corner. She had created an infinite void in his life. A bed made of bamboo was leaning against the wall. A strange thought came to my mind and I started visualizing myself lying on that bed. It would be the last bed for everyone around me, I thought. After several minutes we all left to the cremation Ghat near Ganges. My father and my uncles were shouldering her death bed and I was behind them. We passed through the winding streets to reach the Ganges and she was burned right there. How could I forget that!

It was awfully upsetting. I saw my grandmother burning under the heaps of woods but she wasn't alone, there were innumerable bodies burning around her. A thick smoke hung over the place. Dogs were attentive and on the look to have a piece of charred flesh. A few cows were roaming around to eat the ball of wheat flour that was used for rituals. I saw a flock of vultures hovering over the place. They would dive down briskly into the river and fly away with a fish. I'd never seen a dead body burning and I never knew before that it was so casual a thing there at that place. People were laughing, chatting and were doing their daily routine work. While bringing the body to the river we had gone through many meandering streets and it all seemed surreal.

It was my grandmother's wish that her rituals should be performed in the village. And so we all trooped to our village several kilometers away from the place we were living. There in the village we had a head shave according to the Hindu traditions because my grandmother wished that. Use of razor was prohibited in our family from the time unknown and we were only allowed to use scissors for a haircut. My grandfather didn't want us to do that but we did it against his will. It was then that my friend jolted me back to present.

"Your phone is ringing Nikhil, where are you lost," he said shaking me.

It took me minutes to realize where I was. I wasn't too sure if I was out of dream or not.

I took out my phone and saw my wife's name flashing on the screen. I picked up the call and there was my wife screaming on the other side, her shrill voice pierced through my ears, "She's no more Nikhil, she is no more; I told you not to delay. She needed treatment Nikhil! How young she was, only two months, only two months. How could I ever forgive you?"

I stared back at the screen of my phone; that smile, that captivating face of my daughter was my wallpaper.

She was just two months old, neither a day more nor less.

I asked my friend to pinch me. I wanted him to get me out of this terrible dream. I wanted to get out of this dream we call life.

DEVOTEE

Amidst the heavy hustle and bustle of the city, there's a place that looks like it is still dwelling somewhere in the past. It looks disconnected from the modern world. As you walk past the big orange iron gate you find a place totally impervious to modernity. You'll find old emaciated sadhus with long hair and wooden slippers, long sticks in their hands, roaming around, few cycling alongside the lane, but no one in hurry. There are gigantic trees of neem and mango and on the other side of the narrow path that leads to the main area of the Ashram, there's a huge Banyan tree. There are no crows in the city, and it seems they all have taken a shelter here. When you enter the Ashram's hall, bending head through a small door, you'll see old, damp, black and white wooden framed photos of mystic sadhus, mostly bare bodied with only a loin cloth wrapped around their waists and some even stark naked, hanging everywhere on the wall. On one corner you'll find a few old people listening to a Sadhu well dressed in a neat and clean orange kurta, coughing intermittently, preaching from the Bhagvat Gita placed on a wooden stand in front of him.

However, I had not gone there because I was interested in all these. I went there because my city had no library except the old rustic library of the Ashram. I'd gone there just to take a look at the books they had, though, quite sure about the unavailability of the novels and story books I used to read. They would only have spiritual books, I had thought. I was around 16 when I'd first visited the library. I had no money in my pocket. I had never even thought of taking a membership. It was just in curiosity and because of the abundance of free time I had then, that I took out my bicycle, and squeezed through the heavy traffic to reach there. I was a nature lover and I fell in love with the place at the very first sight. The huge trees and the various birds in the Ashram attracted me a lot. Library was upstairs on the second floor. It was not a very big library, just a tiny room crammed with as many shelves as it could accommodate. There were a table and four chairs in a corner where a young lad was busy binding books. Scissors, glue, thread everything were scattered on the table. There were old books stacked up in one corner, pages eaten by bookworms, a few were torn up from the spine, and many seemed like they could never be repaired. On the left side just beside the library's door, there was one chair and a small table where a Sadhu was sitting. He looked around sixty years old, clean shaven, wrapped in a white cloth with a white cap on his head. There was a book lying face down on the table in front. It was a book by Swami Vivekananda. He had dozed off with his head resting back on the chair. I wanted to take his permission before browsing the books and so I coughed just to make him aware of my presence. However, the man remained unmoved in his slumber. He woke up when the young lad Sumitra who was binding books behind me, came near and whispered at him, "Swami Ji, a boy."

He rubbed his eyes, took his glasses resting over his book on the table, adjusted it over his nose and looked at me with surprise, 'quite young you are,' he said.

"Do you have Tagore's books here?" I asked him, coming straight to the point.

"Introduce yourself first. Don't you think you should greet people you meet for the first time," he said quite harshly.

I was quite taken aback by his unprofessional behavior. I wasn't expecting a librarian to teach me ethics. I was there to read books, not to greet people. However, it was useless to argue and waste time, so I just introduced myself, and I was expecting an introduction in return, but he only ordered me in an authoritative way, 'I'm the librarian, call me Swam Ji.'

He rose from his chair and motioned me to follow him.

"Arvind, we have lots of books here, many from Swami Vivekananda. I hope you'll read all his books. Have you ever read him?" he asked, taking a bunch of keys from a key hanger.

"No, I don't read spiritual books; I'm here to look for storybooks and novels. Do you have Tagore's books Swami Ji?" I asked him again.

He turned around abruptly and smiled, "Arvind why do you want to read Rabindranath Thakur's books so much?"

"Oh! I love his stories; I want to read more of him."

"Good! But you cannot take books to your home unless you're a registered member. Meanwhile, you may read sitting here."

He opened the locks of a few shelves which had books of fiction and went back to his chair.

This was our first meeting. After a week, I begged my mother for hundred rupees and went again to the library to get registered.

I wasn't much eager to get registered, but it was impossible to read there in the library. It wasn't that there was any noise there though. Library remained deserted most of the time. I found no other reader except me. Shopping Malls have gathered attention of youths nowadays. I seemed to be +the youngest person in the vicinity to come here. In fact the place was like something from another world. Inside the ashram you didn't hear honking of horns or the noise created by vehicles, the air was pure and the place was filled with monotonous calls of cuckoo's cooing now and then, but Swami Ji wouldn't leave me alone for a minute. He would come every now and then with some books by Swami Vivekananda and would start reading it to me. He wouldn't let me read any other book.

"Arvind, read this paragraph and tell me what you understand," he would say, and I had to read the books of his choice. There was no escape. He wouldn't let me read anything else and it was impossible to refuse him. He was so authoritative and yet so loving, his patronizing manners towards me, cowed me totally, to do whatever he needed.

So, there was no other way than to borrow some books and read it at home. However, Swami Ji didn't let me do that too. He would issue two books for a month, but there would always be one book of his choice. Of course, they were by Swami Vivekananda. He would also ask me each time I returned the books, "So, did you read the book I gave you," and I would lie that I did, fearing what to say if he asked anything further, but he didn't ask any further. He would abruptly take out a book of Vivekananda from the shelf near his hand, and ask me to read from a page. I would be bored to death as he listened with his eyes shut. I would think he was asleep but the time I stopped, he would open his eyes immediately and say, 'go on, and read further, you're improving.' I would steal furtive glances to the old wooden clock hanging on the wall over his head, worrying that it would soon be the closing time of library and I wouldn't get any time to look for a new book, but he would open his eyes just a few minutes before the closing time, and ask me to browse quickly for the next month. When I returned with a novel, he would already be waiting there with a Vivekananda book, 'read it sincerely this time,' he would say with a pleasant smile on his face.

On some days, when I wouldn't find him in the library, I felt immensely happy. I would feel free and read novels for hours there, but while leaving I felt as if I didn't come to library at all. Library wasn't the same place without him. I was accustomed to his presence and it seemed the library too was.

During those days my biggest sorrow was that the library remained closed for summer vacation, but I did visit Swami Ji at his place. His tiny room had some divine charm. It had a distinct damp smell of old house. There was a thin ragged mat on the ground, and a few utensils and a stove in a corner where he cooked his food. His books were lying next to his pillow, all were by Swami Vivekananda. On the front wall there was a small poster of Swami Vivekananda. An incense stick would always be burning at front. He was surrounded by Swami Vivekananda all over the place and I could bet that nothing else was there in his mind and heart too. Once I asked him, "Swami Ji, do you read nothing except books by Swami Vivekananda?", and he had replied, "There's nothing else in this world dear, Vivekananda told everything. Why to read anything else!"

In one corner his Tanpura was standing against the wall.

"Swami Ji, I didn't know you sing?"

"I don't just sing Arvind, I pray." He had said.

Just next to his Tanpura there was a small wooden stool painted green, over which there was an antique transistor radio in a worn out leather case. Sometimes while cooking he would play it and hum with the old film songs. It was quite strange for me. I didn't know Sadhus sang filmy songs. He told me he loved Mukesh's voice. Swami Ji wasn't pretentious or artful at all. He had no shame in accepting that a man's heart is prone to fall in love and he had fallen in love with Swami Vivekananda.

Once I couldn't go to library for two months due to exams, and when I returned there after exams Swami Ji became angry.

"You are late, thirty days! You'll have to pay late fine. Thirty rupees for thirty days."

I didn't like it coming from Swami Ji. I thought I was a favorite of Swami Ji and he wouldn't ask me for a fine. I was just taking out the money from my pocket when he asked, "do you want to pay fine or donate?"

So now he wants money for himself like all the others, I thought. I thought for a minute or two and said, "I would donate."

"Wise decision! It's better to donate now than to pay fine later. Now run to the donation box downstairs."

I was so ashamed of myself for thinking wrong about Swami Ji. I went downstairs, folded thirty rupees and dropped it in the red donation box.

I soon started touching his feet. With passing years there developed a bond between us. I would also talk about him at home. He didn't know how important he had become in our lives.

Once my mother asked me to invite him for lunch but Swami Ji told me that he only ate food cooked by him.

One day I asked Swami Ji to give me at least one photograph of his. I wanted to keep it with me. He had a place in our lives just like any other family member, but he refused humbly.

"Arvind, why should you take my photo? I don't keep my photos with me. I never took any. I'm not yet the one I want to be. Perhaps I'll take one, one day, when I feel I'm a complete man like Vivekananda. I'll give you my photo then, I promise."

I would visit library daily in the evening, and after the library closed I would walk down to his room with him. I would make tea for him, and lend him a hand in his cooking. He had given me this permission after a lot of insistence. The first thing he did after unlocking the door was light the incense stick in front of the picture. Afterwards, he would do his prayers for what seemed hours to me. Meanwhile, I would flip the pages of the books he had, and would try to concentrate but it seemed too weighty for me. Once, while flipping the pages of one old book I had found a black and white passport size photograph of a young lady. When I asked him he told me that she was his mother but his parents had died long back when he was quite young. He had spent most part of his life as an orphan, without a family, but yet he never looked sad or nostalgic. Perhaps, he considered Swami Vivekananda, to be his family, his only teacher, his only love. During winter when our school remained closed due to extreme cold weather, I would bath early in the morning, comb my hair carefully, put on my sweater and rushed to the Ashram. Swami Ji wasn't like any other Sadhu; he didn't bath very early in the morning, in fact he waited for the sun to come over his head. I would heat some water for him and fetch it to the veranda, and then I would see him bathing for long. He looked so thin bare bodied. From out of his clothes nobody could tell he was so slender, his loose, sagging skin looked like it would burst open at the mere touch. His whole body was wrinkled. On his arms and legs blue veins were bulging out from under his skin. I loved watching him bath. He would mutter his prayers and shiver like a child at the first touch of water. I would lose myself in the time, seeing the tiny droplets shining under the sun on his body, as if it encapsulated the huge sun.

I was two months late this time. I had to prepare for my exams. My parents were worried lest I wouldn't be able to make it to the next semester. A man would never be free from exams. But in those days, it gave me immense pleasure when I came out of the classroom after the last exam, living in illusion that all exams were over.

I was all prepared. I knew Swami Ji would be furious. I knew he would ask me to choose between paying fine or donating. I had money in my pocket. I decided that I would donate before meeting Swami Ji. It would make him happy, I had thought. I parked my bicycle near the banyan tree, tied it to a pole with a chain and headed towards the Ashram hall. I strode over to the red tin box and dropped thirty rupees in it and then headed towards the stairs. I was just climbing the stairs to library when Sumitra who used to bind books there met me in the middle of the stairs, and gave me the most heart-breaking news of my life. I had never even dreamt of that. Swami Ji was perfectly healthy the last time I had met him. But a human's life is like this. Nobody knows who will be vanished from the face of this earth the next day.

I shuddered at the mere thought of Swami Ji's death.

I couldn't believe my ears. I asked the boy to repeat his words and at the same time I didn't want to hear him at all. I shook myself hoping it might be a nightmare. But, life is sometimes worse than your wildest nightmares.

"Arvind, Swami Ji left a letter for you," was the next voice I vaguely heard from Sumitra.

I tried to collect myself, but it was difficult. I felt broken and my eyes were unable to see anything. My hands were shivering as I tried to grab the letter. I wiped my face which was drenched with tears by then, and opened the letter with my fumbling hands.

Letter read as follows:

"Dear Arvind, I've been feeling as if I'm complete for the last few days. I feel better and I can see my Guru Swami Vivekananda sitting by my pillow and caressing me in the nights. I've never felt this happiness before. It's a state of ecstasy. I know you never read Vivekananda but please take the keys from Sumitra, and take my books from my room and keep it safe. I know you would read him one day. I wouldn't be here for long. I wish you come before I depart this life and this body. I remember once you'd asked for my photo. I have given it to Sumitra. Please take it from him. Don't be sad if you don't find me in my old body. There's nothing strange in dying. It happens and it will always happen. I feel like I have wings and I'm flying. I leave my blessings for you."

I was crying relentlessly after reading this. I hadn't noticed that I was holding another folded paper along with the letter. Now I knew it was his photo, 'your Swami ji' was written in the middle, and I unfolded it.

It was the same poster of Swami Vivekananda he had on his wall.

Perhaps, it was his message to tell me, what it's like to be a complete man. What one should try to be equal to.

Now I have the same Swami Vivekananda photo in my room stuck to the front wall, and through him I find my Swami Ji.

www.ingramcontent.com/pod-product-compliance
Lightning Source LLC
Chambersburg PA
CBHW020755130626
46554CB00006B/2196